Sloths
Don't Run

To Rowan, may you always find the courage to chase your dreams.

Sloths
Don't Run

by Tori McGee

illustrated by Roksolana Panchyshyn

Somewhere in the rainforest,

high up in a tree,

there lives a pleasant sloth named Hank

and a clever moth named Dee.

They live their lives quite leisurely,

sleeping lots and moving slow.

They climb down from their tall tree home

once every week or so.

Hank's always been quite happy

with this laid-back style of living,

but lately he's been thinking

that there might be something missing.

While moving slow and sleeping

is how most sloths spend their days,

recently Hank asked himself,

"Could I maybe change my ways?"

You see, Hank knows that sloths
aren't the most athletic creatures.
He wonders though, "Could I go fast,
with training and some sneakers?"

One day while hanging in the tree,

Hank makes a big decision.

He's nervous of what Dee might think,

but decides to share his vision.

"All day I watch the jaguars

as they run from place to place.

This year I'd like to join them

for The Great Rainforest Race."

Dee isn't sure of Hank's grand plan;

she says it's a no-go.

"Hank, it's not a good idea.

Sloths don't run! Didn't you know?"

Sure, jaguars are natural athletes,

and they seem to move with ease.

"But with practice I can do it," Hank claims.

"Come with me, Dee, won't you please?"

Hank climbs down slowly from his tree,

gripping tightly with his claws.

Then he laces up all four sneakers—

one shoe for each of his paws.

Dee isn't sure about Hank's plan,

but now what can she say?

She decides that she'll support her friend,

each step along the way.

And so begins Hank's training

for his big rainforest run,

but unlike the sporty jaguars,

Hank isn't having any fun.

"This running stuff is such hard work.

I'm tired," Hank says to Dee.

"I think I'll jog just a bit more,

then we'll head back to the tree."

Each day Hank and Dee come down

to practice for the race.

Eventually Hank finds the joy

along with his happy pace.

It's here! It's here! Today's the day!

The Great Rainforest Race!

The animals toe the starting line.

Hank and Dee each take their place.

The toucan shouts, "Ready, Set, Go!"

and the animals take off fast.

Hank and Dee start slowly;

other racers run right past.

The jaguars take off in a hurry;

the monkeys aren't far behind.

As the animals come racing by,

only finishing is on Hank's mind.

Hank knows this slow and steady pace

will get them to the line.

So they press on toward the finish,

taking one step at a time.

Midway they fall into last place;

they're on the course alone.

But that doesn't matter much to them;

They're in a race of their own.

They inch their way toward the finish,

slow and steady as they've been.

And in the end they're greeted

with their very own kind of win.

You see, they didn't finish first.

In fact, they took last place.

But they learned an important lesson—

more important than any race!

Hank learned a lesson in courage—

that it comes straight from the heart.

And Dee learned that sometimes winning

is having the courage to start.

Later they returned up high

to a life of leisure in their tree.

On nice days they still go jogging,

just Hank and his pal Dee.

Made in the USA
Monee, IL
19 January 2021